I0669697

C. S. Smith

The life of Daniel Alexander Payne, D.D., LL.D.

C. S. Smith

The life of Daniel Alexander Payne, D.D., LL.D.

ISBN/EAN: 9783741114878

Manufactured in Europe, USA, Canada, Australia, Japa

Cover: Foto ©Andreas Hilbeck / pixelio.de

Manufactured and distributed by brebook publishing software
(www.brebook.com)

C. S. Smith

The life of Daniel Alexander Payne, D.D., LL.D.

A MONOGRAPH.

THE LIFE

OF

Daniel Alexander Payne, D. D., LL. D.

BY

REV. C. S. SMITH, D. D.,

WITH AN INTRODUCTION

BY

BISHOP ABRAM GRANT, D D.,

AND A POEM, "IN MEMORIAM,"

BY

BISHOP JAS. A. HANDY, D. D.

———

NASHVILLE, TENN.:
PUBLISHING HOUSE A. M. E. CHURCH SUNDAY SCHOOL UNION.
1894.

RT. REV DANIEL ALEXANDER PAYNE, D. D., LL. D.

PREFACE.

The task involved in the preparation of this Monograph is one of love and grateful remembrance of a devoted benefactor. For eleven years, three months and seventeen days Bishop Payne and myself were officially related in connection with the work of the African Methodist Episcopal Church Sunday School Union, he serving as its President, and I as its Corresponding Secretary and Treasurer. During this time I came to know something of his exalted character, something of those excellent qualities which made his name a synonym for uprightness and righteousness. From the hour that our official relation was first formed until death severed it, I never had cause to complain of his manner toward me or his treatment of me. And it is with inexpressible pleasure I now state that during our official relation for upwards of eleven years, there never existed a single difference or disagreement between us. We worked together with single concord of spirit and oneness of aim, and the success which the Sunday School Union of the African Methodist Episcopal Church has achieved is very largely due to Bishop Payne's unswerving fidelity to duty as its first and only President, until the time of his death, and to his just and generous treatment of me as its chief executive officer.

(4)

INTRODUCTION.

No one perhaps is better prepared to write a Monograph on the life of the late Bishop Daniel A. Payne, D. D., LL. D., than Rev C. S. Smith, D. D., whose devoted friendship for the Bishop, growing out of a number of years of close official relationship, warrants him that knowledge which an eager public solicits of the character of one who was held in such high esteem as was Bishop Payne.

There will be a demand for this Monograph on the life of the oldest Bishop in the A. M. E. Church, and the one who held the office of a Bishop longer than any one who has yet occupied the episcopal chair in any branch of the Methodist family It will not only be appreciated by those who knew him, and who learned to love him as he mingled with them in their social and religious life, but by those also who, reading it, will be inspired to make their "lives sublime, and departing, leave behind them," as he did, "footprints on the sands of time."

The object of this book is to give a fair knowledge of the inner life of this noble divine, as seen from different phases, and a general impression of his work, together with extracts from his able productions. To be without it is to deprive one's self of the means of a fair and satisfactory knowledge of one of the greatest teachers

and preachers of the nineteenth century The author
no doubt esteems the preparation of this volume as
one of the greatest privileges of his life, and is made
to rejoice that he can pay this tribute to the memory
of a cherished friend, who, " though dead, yet speaketh."

A. GRANT.

Atlanta, Ga., January 6, 1894.

CONTENTS.

Section.		Page.
I.	Parentage and Ancestry	9
II.	Childhood and Youth	12
III.	Student Days	14
IV.	Work as an Educator	18
V.	Pastoral Labors	26
VI.	Episcopal Functions	29
VII.	A Patron of Music and Literature	33
VIII.	Literary Productions	36
IX.	Travels	42
X.	As a Citizen	45
XI.	Home Life	48
XII.	Moral and Religious Character	52
XIII.	Funeral Services	55

IN MEMORIAM.

Bishop Daniel Alexander Payne, D. D., LL. D.

BY BISHOP JAS. A. HANDY, D. D.

Come, ye sighing prelates of sorrow,
  View with me our colleague's tomb :
Learn from it our fate : to-morrow,
  Death, perhaps, may seal our doom.

Sad and solemn flows our numbers,
  While disconsolate we mourn
The loss of him who sweetly slumbers,
  Mouldering neath the silent urn.

May we all, his hope possessing,
  Triumphant leave the Church below ;
Crowned with everlasting blessing,
  Far removed from pain and woe.

Once, when full of life, he never
  Proved unfaithful to our laws :
May we, like him, be zealous, ever,
  To promote this glorious cause.

To the exalted power Almighty,
  Softly breathe an ardent prayer ;
On his sacred mound tread lightly,
  While we wipe the falling tear.

Kansas City, Kan., Dec. 26th, 1893.

(8)

The Life of Daniel Alexander Payne.

PARENTAGE AND ANCESTRY.

Daniel Alexander Payne, D. D., L. L. D., was the only son of London and Martha Payne. His father is said to have been of brown complexion, slender in form, five feet eight inches high. It has been stated that he was born of free parents in the state of Virginia, but when a mere boy was decoyed on board a ship and carried to Charleston. where he was sold as a slave to a painter. He remained in this condition until he reached manhood, when he purchased his freedom for $1,000. He belonged to the Methodist Church, and filled the position of class-leader for a considerable time He was free and faithful in the exercise of the means of grace, and was a strict observer of family worship. Information has been given that he was one of six brothers who served in the American Revolutionary War.

Daniel's great-grandfather was an Englishman by the name of Paine. The change of *i* to *y*, the latter

(9)

being used to spell the name of Daniel's ancestry, grew out of the fact that his great-grandfather and one of his brothers were among the early emigrants from England to Massachusetts; and as the former decided to go as a colonist to Jamestown, Va., and the latter concluded to remain in Massachusetts, the two agreed to change the letter *i* to *y* in the name of the one who resolved to go to Virginia, in order that his descendants might be identified separate and apart from the descendants of the one who determined to remain in Massachusetts.

His mother was of a light brown complexion, medium stature, and delicate frame. She was an admixture of African and Indian; the African coming down through her grandfather's side and the Indian through her mother's side. Her grandmother was of the tribe of Indians known as the "Catawbas." Her grandfather, Alexander Goins, a black man, was remarkable for great strength and activity.

The admixture of African and Indian blood which flowed through the veins of Daniel A. Payne may, to some extent, account for certain peculiarities of temperament. Two of his most striking peculiarities were distrust and resentment. There were very few persons in whom he confided. It is doubtful whether he ever communicated his inner thoughts to any one. He had no confidants. Perhaps, it may be true that the frequency of deception which had been practiced upon him by many of his fellows was one of the causes of his distrust; it may also be assigned to the presence of Indian blood as one of the elements of his physical composition, as distrust is one of the strong characteristics of the Indian. His disposition to resentment was forcible and emphatic. He could not brook opposition with patience. To oppose him, was to instantly kindle the fire of itense resentment in every fiber of his body, mind and soul.

When thus aroused, he was passionate, vehement, and inclined to be revengeful. While in some cases this exhibition of feeling was but transient, in others it seemed to be permanent and abiding. Many have wondered why such strong resentment should be possessed by one whose piety was so deep and fervent that at times his very countenance seemed to be illuminated with angelic brightness. Many of those who thus wondered were doubtless unmindful of the teachings of human experience that ofttimes while the spirit is willing the flesh is weak, and that grace is not bestowed to uproot all natural impulses and propensities. It is given to restrain, and yet there seem to be some impulses which are stronger, to exemplify, as it were, that in all lines of human conduct, " There is none perfect, no not one." His disposition to resentment, like that of distrust, may be attributed to the presence of the Indian blood in his veins. It is well that the fiery and revengeful propensity of the Indian blood in him was strongly offset by the docility and gentleness of the African blood. I may not be justified in saying that the admixture of the blood of these two varieties of the human race was a happy union, but I do say, that it was productive of strong qualities of character, which bore fruits of pleasing aspects and abundant blessings.

CHILDHOOD AND YOUTH.

His childhood days, until he was within six months of the tenth year of his age, were passed under the parental care of his mother, aided by that of his father, until the first four and a half years of his being; when, as previously stated, his father died. His parents possessing devout and pious dispositions, it is safe to infer that they exercised due diligence in striving to train up their son in the nurture and admonition of the Lord. After the death of his father it was the custom of his mother to take him to class-meeting with her. This she was evidently prompted to do by

MR. SAMUEL WATSON,
Bishop Payne's First Class Leader—the Bishop
Joined the Methodist Church in His
Fifteenth Year.

the feeling that she alone was responsible to God for the religious instruction of her boy. She did not, as many mothers of this day do, deem it a burden to take her children with her to the house of worship.

After the death of his mother he was placed in charge of a grandaunt by the name of Mrs. Sarah Bordeaux, who happily was zealous in stimulating him to attain unto a noble character. It will thus be seen that despite the deep, dark shadows which were thrown across his pathway by the death of his parents in early life, there was a divinity which was shaping his ends.

The days of his youth were chiefly spent in acquiring a knowledge of industrial pursuits. In the twelfth year of his age he was hired out to a shoe-merchant, with whom he did not remain very long.

When about thirteen years of age he was apprenticed to learn the carpenter's trade with his brother in-law, Mr. James Holloway, with whom he remained four and a half years. Subsequent to this he spent nine months at the tailor's trade. Thus, for nearly six years of his youth he labored with his hands and provided his own support. The knowledge which he gained of the shoe business, carpenter's and tailor's trades, was of great value to him throughout after life.

He knew just what material to order when he wanted
a pair of boots, or a suit of clothes made. He always
preferred boots to shoes, and seldom, if ever, wore the
latter. His knowledge of the carpenter's trade was in-
valuably helpful to him, when, in 1845, he designed
the plan for the erection of Bethel Church, Baltimore,
Md. This edifice, at the time of its erection, was, and,
in fact, is now, the most substantial church edifice
possessed by colored people in America. Its exterior,
which is of great plainness and simplicity, is in striking contrast with its interior. Elder Payne, for that
was his title in 1845, was of a decidedly practical turn
of mind. He did not believe in lavishing money on
the exterior of church edifices, so that when he came
to plan for Bethel, he did not include stone trimmings.
gothic form, a belfry or a spire for the exterior. He
aimed at solidity at every point, and provided for the
beautifying of the interior. He built a structure that
will endure for ages, and in its interior arrangement
and adornment, will ever prove pleasing to the eye.
It is no impoverishment of one's accomplishments to
have a knowledge of industrial pursuits.

STUDENT DAYS.

His career as a student is, indeed, most interesting
and remarkable. No man of any age, of any variety

of the human race, or clime, ever studied more method-
ically than what he did, or pursued systematic study
with more uniformity and persistency If asked how
long he was a student, the reply might justly be given
— his entire life.   Let us notice some particulars.

When about eight years old he entered a school
which was supported by the Minor's Moralist Society,
for the care and education of orphan and indigent colored children.   This society was founded in 1803 in
the city of Charleston by James Mitchell, Joseph
Humphreys, William Cooper, Carlow Hugher, Thomas
S. Bonneau, William Clark and Richard Holloway—all
free colored men.   The society continued its existence
until 1847, when it was disbanded.   It is indeed striking that such a society should exist in a slave city at
such an early date.   It is true that it was established
by colored men who were free; but who, though free,
were, nevertheless, hampered and restricted in their
movements and means of earning a living by the influences of slavery.   Their charitable disposition is
quite in contrast with that of the colored people of
this day—all of whom are free.   There is not an in-
stitution in America for the care and education of orphan and indigent colored children that has been
founded and maintained through the charity and

philanthropy of any colored man or men. If there is any exception to this general statement, I shall be glad to have some one inform me of it. Young Daniel was a protege of this society for two years, during which time he showed himself to be an apt and observing pupil. After leaving the school he received private instruction for about three years from a Mr. Thomas Bonneau, one of the founders of the Minor's Moralist Society. During this period he made rapid progress in the rudiments of orthography, reading, writing and arithmetic. Monographs of the histories of Greece Rome and England, were mostly used for exercises in reading. The "Columbian Orator" was the book used for studying rhetorical style and expression. The end of the three years under Mr. Bonneau's tutorship closed the second course of his regular instruction.

During the nearly six years he was engaged in manual avocation, he prosecuted his studies with great earnestness and zeal. He studied with great interest a book called the "Self-interpreting Bible," by the Rev. John Brown, of Haddington, Scotland. The book was prefaced with a biographical sketch of the author, the reading of which became the turning point in Daniel's life. He was profoundly impressed with the noble character and matchless learning of the Rev. John Brown, who seemed to have become thoroughly versed in Hebrew, Greek and Latin, without the aid of a teacher. Daniel becoming inspired with the patience and fortitude manifested by the learned author, resolved to try to be like him in character and learning. After this he read many books, among which was the " Scottish Chiefs, " which filled him with enthusiasm as he marked the boldness and courage displayed by Wallace and Bruce, and they became his ideal great men. He devoted every spare moment to the study of books, and every cent to the purchase of them. He raised money for this purpose by making tables, benches, clothes-horses and corset-bones, which he sold on Saturday in the public market. While serving at the carpenter's trade he would begin his studies at four o'clock in the morning, would resume them at the close of the day's work and continue until midnight. He always kept a tinderbox, flint, steel and candle at his bedside. He would relieve himself at times of the strain of continued study by drawing pictures with crayon and composing verses. At one time his life's work as an educator came near being thwarted. He had heard of Hayti and its people, and was seized with a desire to go there as a soldier. This purpose, however, was dissipated by the influence of a dream in which he beheld all the horrors of war.

His third course of regular instruction was received in a Lutheran college at Gettysburg, Pa., which he entered June, 1835, where he remained two years, when he was forced to discontinue his studies by reason of failing eyesight. His studies while at Gettysburg were chiefly in the field of Theology, though he studied German, Mental Philosophy and Archaeology, in addition to the curriculum of the Theological Seminary While at Gettysburg he contributed to his own support by cutting wood, cleaning boots and shaving. What courage! What self-reliance!

WORK AS AN EDUCATOR.

Daniel A. Payne was a born educator. He tells us that shortly after his conversion, which took place in his eighteenth year, that one day while engaged in his noon hour devotions, he seemed to feel the hands of a man pressing upon his shoulders, and a voice speaking within his soul, saying: " I have set thee apart to educate thyself in order that thou mayst be an educator of thy people." The impression was irresistible and gave a new direction to his thoughts and efforts. He entered upon his life's work as an educator at the age of eighteen years.

Schoolhouse Built for Bishop Payne by Mr. Robert Howard
in 1830, on Anson Street, Charleston, S. C.

His first school was opened in 1829, in a house on
Tradd Street, which was occupied by one Cæsar
Wright. His first pupils were Mr. Wright's three children, for whose instruction he received fifty cents each
per month. He also taught a night school of three
pupils, who were adult slaves. From these he received
fifty cents each per month, making his total month-
ly income three dollars. His income was supple-
mented by the favors of a slave woman, who furnished
him food and other necessaries. His day school increased in numbers until the room in which he was
teaching became too small to accommodate his schol-
ars. Another room was obtained, but this in time also
became too small. A friend of his, by the name of
Mr. Robert Howard, provided larger and more suitable
accommodations for his school, by the erection of a
schoolhouse in the rear of his yard, on Anson Street.
This was, perhaps, the first schoolhouse for colored
children erected by a colored man in America. It
was built in 1830. Here he continued to teach until
1835.

After six years of successful effort in school teaching, and with the future radiant with the promise
and hope of greater success, a cloud of dark and
portentious aspect suddenly arose. The General

Assembly of South Carolina legislated the teacher's
rod out of his hands by enacting the following law,
which went into effect April 1st, 1835 :

No. 2639.

An Act to Amend the Law Relating to Slaves and Free Persons of
Color.

Be it enacted, by the honorable, the Senate and House of Rep-
resentatives, now met and sitting in General Assembly, and by the
authority of the same: If any person shall hereafter teach any
slave to read or write, or cause, or procure any slave to read or
write, such person, if a free white person, upon conviction thereof
shall for each and every offense against this Act be fined not exceeding one hundred dollars and imprisoned not more than six
months ; or, if a free person of color, shall be whipped not exceeding fifty lashes and fined not exceeding fifty dollars, at the discre-
tion of the court of magistrates and free-holders before which such
person of color is tried ; and, if a slave, to be whipped at the dis-
cretion of the court, not exceeding fifty lashes ; the informer to be
entitled to one-half of the fine, and to be a competent witness.
And, if any free person of color or slave shall keep any school or
other place of instruction for teaching any slave or free person of
color or slave, shall be liable to the same fine, imprisonment, and
corporal punishment as are by this Act imposed and inflicted upon
free persons of color and slaves for teaching slaves to read or
write.

The effect of the passage of this Act on Schoolmaster Payne's mind was withering and blighting. Sleep
fled from his eyes and he dreaded the night. In fact,

this viper of cruel and unjust legislation had plunged
its fangs so deeply into his heart that he began to
question the existence of God. He was comforted,
however, and his faith securely anchored to its moor-
ings by a still small voice, which said: " With God,
one day is as a thousand years and a thousand years
as one day. Trust in Him, and He will bring slavery
and all its outrages to an end." He then took his pen
and wrote a poem of twenty-three double quatrain
stanzas, giving it the title of " The Mournful Lute or
the Preceptor's Farewell." The following are the last
four stanzas :

> " As when a deer does in the pasture graze,
> The lion roars—she's filled with wild amaze,
> Knows strength unequal for the dreadful fight,
> And seeks sweet safety in her rapid flight—
> So Payne prepares to leave his native home,
> With pigmy purse on distant shores to roam.
> Lo! in the skies my boundless storehouse is !
> I go reclining on God's promises:
>
> " Pupils, attend my last departing sounds ;
> Ye are my hopes, and ye my mental crowns,
> My monuments of intellectual might,
> My robes of honor and my armor bright.
> Like Solomon, entreat the throne of God ;
> Light shall descend in lucid columns broad,

And all that man has learned or man can know
In streams prolific shall your minds o'erflow.

" Hate sin ; love God ; religion be your prize ;
Her laws obeyed will surely make you wise,
Secure you from the ruin of the vain,
And save your souls from everlasting pain.
O, fare you well for whom my bosom glows
With ardent love, which Christ my Saviour knows!
'Twas for your good I labored night and day ;
For you I wept, and now for you I pray.

" Farewell ! farewell ! ye children of my love ,
May joys abundant flow ye from above!
May peace celestial crown your useful days,
To bliss transported, sing eternal lays ;
For sacred wisdom give a golden world,
And when foul vice his charming folds unfurl,
O spurn the monster, though his crystal eyes
Be like bright sunbeams streaming from the skies !
And I ! O whither shall your tutor fly ?
Guide thou my feet, great Sovereign of the sky."

Thus stunned and hampered, Schoolmaster Payne
resolved to go North in search of a new field of labor
Securing letters of recommendation from a number of
Charleston's distinguished citizens to eminent citizens
of New York City, he set sail from the former city for
the latter Saturday, May 9th, 1835, about four o'clock
p. m., arriving in New York the following Wednesday

The following testimonial now published for the first time, was given him by the patrons of his school :

(A TRUE COPY OF THE ORIGINAL.)

CHARLESTON, S. C., May 8th, 1835.

At a meeting of those parents that had children under the tuition of Mr. D. A. Payne, held the 31st of March, 1835,

The following Preamble and Resolutions were submitted and unanimously concurred in :

It is with regret and dismay these Parents who had children under the Tuition of Mr. Payne, having witnessed for several successive days these exercises in the different branches of an English Education, and sympathizing deeply in the loss our children has sustained in an efficient Teacher, fills us at once with deep sorrow. Had we been deprived of him by the ordinary course of Nature, as a Christian duty, we would humbly submit to the Divine will ; but no, Carolina's late Act has deprived the Colored man from imparting mental Instruction to his own race, and our friend has to seek a home elsewhere in order that he may continue to Instruct the Colored Youth.

It was our happy lot to have witnessed the pleasing and gratifying sight of the only school in this state (come into existence), where the Elementary Branches of an English Education are taught and the Teacher a colored man—D. A. Payne, and he self-taught, and an orphan at a very early age, and unaided by fortune. His piety, talent, general good conduct, his manners and his great zeal for improving his people, have secured for him the esteem and respect of all whom knew him. To us as Parents he is equally dear. But, as we said in the foregoing, he is about to seek

a home in another land. Painful as is the separation which will
shortly take place between our friend and us, yet the hope of meeting even in a better world cheers us in this great affliction. Go on,
our children's Friend: Carry with you our Thanks, our gratitude,
our good wishes. Our prayers to Heaven shall always resound for
your present and eternal welfare, wherever your lot may be Cast
Heaven's choicest blessing attend you. May abundant success crown
your every effort, and as a Testimonial of our confidence for your
good character, great ability to teach, and earnest zeal for the im
provement of our children,

Be it Resolved :

That the meeting of Parents do hereby recommend Mr. D. A.
Payne as a Teacher of Youth and in every way worthy of being
encouraged in that employment.

And further Resolved :

That this meeting do earnestly solicit in the behalf of our friend
the influence and the zeal of the Colored Brethern in establishing
him in a school.

Resolved :

That the above Preamble and Resolutions be signed by the President and Secretary of this meeting.

THOS INGLES, Pres.
JOHN MISHAW, Sec.

He resumed his work as an educator in Philadelphia in 1840, on Fourth Street, near Spruce. He began with three pupils, the same number with which he
opened his school in Charleston, ten years previously
His work in Philadelphia, as an educator, was highly

successful. There were two select schools in existence when he opened his, but within one year he had absorbed both of them. He taught until 1843, when he joined the itinerant ministry of the African Methodist Episcopal Church. In 1845 he again performed the duties of a schoolmaster in Baltimore, Md., in which city he was then serving as a pastor. He taught at this place at intervals for about five years.

In 1863, when Wilberforce University, at Tawawa Springs, O., was purchased from the Methodist Episcopal Church for the African Methodist Episcopal Church, Bishop Payne, for he had then been a Bishop since 1852, was elected its President, though he did not enter upon the active discharge of the duties of his position until 1865. Into the success of Wilberforce University he put all the strength of his heart, mind and soul. He was one of the trustees and a member of the Executive Board of the University throughout the entire period that it was in the possession of the M. E. Church. From the time of its purchase by the A. M. E. Church until the hour of his death he held some position in connection with it, being at the time of his decease its Chancellor and the Dean of its Theological Department. Eternity alone can reveal the measure of the influences which he exerted for the development and prosperity of the University, as well as the number of youths whose minds he assisted in enlightening, and whose lives he helped to shape in the mould of correct thinking and upright living.

PASTORAL LABORS.

His pastoral career was brief, onerous and trying, but successful. The first pastoral service which he rendered was in connection with a Presbyterian church in East Troy, New York. This was in June, 1837, and in the twenty-sixth year of his age. His pastoral labors at Troy extended through a period of less than two years, owing to a serious throat affection which compelled him to discontinue preaching. In the spring of 1842 he joined the Philadelphia Annual Conference of the A. M. E. Church, and in May, 1843, was appointed to the pastoral charge of Israel Church, Washington, D. C., where he served with great success, for two years. While in Washington he organized the first Pastoral Association among colored preachers. In 1845 he assumed charge of Bethel A. M. E. Church, Baltimore, Md., where he remained for five years. This was the last charge he held prior to his election to the bishopric in 1852. The five years that he spent in Baltimore were perhaps the saddest and most try-

ing of all the years of his life. The place seemed to
be the mount of temptation and assault—temptation
to forswear his ministerial vows, and assault unjust
and violent.

When he assumed the pastoral charge of Bethel,
Baltimore, it consisted of three societies—Bethel, Ebenezer, and Union Bethel. The property used by
Ebenezer society belonged to Bethel, and was entirely
incommodious and sadly in need of repairs. The
trustees of Bethel, however, would not consent to have
the property remodeled or enlarged. Pastor Payne
advised Ebenezer society to submit a proposition for
the purchase of the property. This it did, and the
trustees of Bethel named four thousand dollars as the
price. This price Pastor Payne strenuously opposed
as being too exorbitant, and without any consideration,
for the fact that the members of Ebenezer were poorer
than the members of Bethel, and that the adherents
of both societies were bound together by kindred ties
and religious fellowship. He said : " We should require them to pay only a ten dollar bill, and let them
have the four thousand dollars for needed improve-
ments." The trustees of Bethel would not listen to
this suggestion and the matter was submitted to the
members, a majority of whom voted in the affirma-

tive. Thus did Ebenezer come in possession of valable property for the nominal sum of ten dollars. The trustees of Bethel, or at least a number of them, never became reconciled to this action, and exerted every means to produce dissension and to neutralize Pastor Payne's influence. The galling yoke, though, which was fastened upon his neck, was that of a savage attack which was made by an infuriated woman with a club. He dodged the blow, which glanced off of his shoulder without inflicting serious injury.

The trouble was caused by Pastor Payne's endeavors to modify certain extravagances in worship. He strenuously opposed the singing of "cornfield ditties" and the ludicrous actions of the "Praying and Singing Bands." In this he met with counter opposition on the part of the great majority of the members. It was a conflict between ignorance and intelligence—between a rational conception of the true forms of religious worship and a mere fanciful emotion. Then, as now, ignorance, though it had the strength of numbers on its side, could not triumph over intelligence. In all the eternity of eternities the divine plan, after which all systems have been constructed, will never be so reversed as to cause darkness to be more glorious than light, and error more potent than truth. Pastor Payne emerged from the conflict with the strength of a valiant knight and his labors were ultimately crowned with success.

In 1850 Bishop Quinn appointed him to the pastoral charge of Ebenezer, but the society refused to receive him ; notwithstanding that less than five years previouly he had championed their cause against the exactions of the trustees of Bethel Church, and secured them the property which they had so long desired for a mere pittance. Well, has some one said that, " Ingratitude is the basest of crimes."

EPISCOPAL FUNCTIONS.

In May, 1852, the General Conference of the African Methodist Episcopal Church, in session in Philadelphia, Pa., elevated Pastor Payne to the bishopric. The election took place on the 7th. He began the exercise of his episcopal functions by assuming charge of the first episcopal district, which embraced the Philadelphia Annual Conference and all the New England States. He held the Philadelphia Conference in May, and in June went to New Bedford, Mass., and organized the New England Conference, of which the Rev. T. M. D. Ward, afterwards Bishop Ward, was the secretary.

In 1854 he was assigned to the second district, which embraced the Baltimore and New York Conferences.

At this period an episcopal term extended through
two years, instead of four as now, and the matter of
assignments rested entirely with the bishops. This
was determined at the annual meeting of the Bishops'
Council, the first session of which was held at the
close of the General Conference of 1852, and was
doubtless the result of Bishop Payne's sagacity. He
appreciated the maxim that, "In the multitude of
counsel there is wisdom."

The General Conference of 1856, having abolished
the episcopal district plan, by ordering the bishops to
rotate, from that period until 1860, Bishop Payne exercised his episcopal functions in various parts of the
Connection. Two important events took place in
which he was an actor—the dissolving of the A. M. E.
Church in Canada and the organization of the British
M. E. Church in its stead, and a visit to New Orleans.
The first took place in September, 1856, and the latter
in December of the same year. He exhibited great
courage in going to New Orleans, as at the time of his
visit the whole country was convulsed with anti-
slavery excitement, growing out of the struggle for the
admission of Kansas into the Union as a free state. In
March, 1860, while journeying from Xenia, O., to
Baltimore, Md., he and his traveling companion, the

WILBERFORCE UNIVERSITY IN 1864.

Rev. James Lynch, were rudely thrust from a sleeping car, though they had secured berths before embarking.

The period between 1860 and 1864 was one of great activity with Bishop Payne. The eleventh session of the General Conference convened in Pittsburg, Pa., May 7, 1860. On the 11th of June, 1863, he, in connection with Rev. James A. Shorter (afterwards Bishop Shorter) and Prof. J. G. Mitchell, now Vice-Dean of Payne Theological Seminary, consummated the arrangements for the purchase of Wilberforce University. This was an important movement, and one which has produced most beneficial results. November, 1863, in company with Revs. A. W Wayman and J. M. Brown, both of whom were subsequently elected to the bishopric, he visited Norfolk and Portsmouth, Va. Several points of interest were viewed, among them the encampment of the First Regiment of United States Colored Troops, and the schools conducted by the American Missionary Society. At Norfolk they met the military governor, Brigadier-General James Barnes, who gave Bishop Payne a general letter of introduction to the military commanders in the valley of the Mississippi. In December of the same year, Bishop Payne went to Nashville, Tenn., where he organized two A. M. E. Church societies.

The year 1864 was fraught with interest, as the month of May was the time for the convening of the twelfth session of the General Conference. During this session the first official steps were taken, looking toward the union of the A. M. E. and the A. M. E. Zion Churches, and a document was adopted recommending Bishop Payne to the people of Great Britain as the accredited agent of the A. M. E. Church.

The most striking event which took place in Bishop Payne's career, in the period between 1864-8, was his return to his native city, after an absence of thirty years, for the purpose of re-establishing the A. M. E. Church. May 15, 1865, he organized the South Carolina Annual Conference. May 9, 1866, he left Wilmington, N C., for Savannah, Ga , where he organized the Georgia Annual Conference.

The first part of the period between 1868-72 was spent in Europe, while the latter part was devoted to the discharge of episcopal duties. From 1872 to 1876 he devoted a large share of his time to his duties as the President of Wilberforce University From 1876 to 1880 he had the superintendency of the first episcopal district, embracing the Philadelphia, New York, New Jersey and New England Annual Conferences. From 1880 to 1884 he superintended the second episcopal district, embracing the Baltimore, Virginia and North Carolina Annual Conferences. August 11th, 1882, he assumed the presidency of the Sunday School Union of the A. M. E. Church, a position which he held at the time of his demise. From 1884 to 1888 he had charge of the work in Alabama and Florida, and from 1888 to the time of his death he was in charge of the Ohio, North Ohio and Pittsburg Annual Conferences. Thus did he round up an episcopal career extending through a period of forty-one years six months and thirteen days—dating from May 16th, 1852, the time of his consecration.

A PATRON OF MUSIC AND LITERATURE.

Bishop Payne was an earnest and enthusiastic patron of music and literature. He was the first to introduce choral singing in the African Methodist Episcopal Church, which he did in Bethel Church in Philadelphia, Pa., between 1841-42. This act gave great offense to the older members, especially those who had professed personal sanctification. They said: " You have brought the devil in the church, and, therefore, we will go out." Many of these suited their actions to their words, went out and never returned.

He was also the first to introduce instrumental music in the African Methodist Episcopal Church. This

he did in the years 1848-49 in Bethel church, Baltimore, Md.   During his pastorate to that congregation
a church edifice was erected at a cost of about $15,500.
Immediately after its dedication dissensions arose
among the officers.   At the time of its dedication
$5,000 had been paid, and the remainder was provided
for by the issuance of eight notes of equal amount, to
be paid annually   The dissensions, however, which
had arisen among the officers, rendered the payment
of the first note uncertain.   To overcome this, Pastor
Payne arranged for a grand concert of sacred music,
under the management of Dr. James Fleet, of Georgetown, D. C.   The lyrics were composed by himself in
order, as he said, " that nothing incongruous in sen-
timent to the sanctuary should go in them."   The concert was a success, the net proceeds amounting to
$300. A second concert of the same kind was given for
a similar purpose, the chief feature of which was an
orchestra of seven stringed instruments.   The financial success of these two concerts, as well as the instruction and entertainment they afforded those who
attended them, convinced the members of Bethel
church, that instrumental music could be as fully
consecrated to the services of Almighty God under the
New Testament dispensation as it was under the Old.

Touching the power and efficiency of choral music, Pastor Payne says, "Two things are essential to the saving power and efficiency of choral music—a scientific training and an earnest Christianity. Two things are necessary to make choral singing always profitable to a church—the congregation should always join in singing with the choir, and they should always sing with the spirit and the understanding."

As an earnest and enthusiastic patron of choral and instrumental music, Pastor Payne has left his impress upon the entire Connection ; there being to-day, without a single exception, not an African Methodist Episcopal Church congregation in any city, town or village, but what aspires to the possession of an organ and the service of a well-trained choir.

His earnestness and enthusiasm for the progress of literature was as great, if not greater, than that for the development of sacred music. He not only kept pace with the onward flow and progressive movements in the world of letters, but encouraged scores of young men and women in and out of the Church to do likewise. He not only encouraged the young, but urged the old to increase their knowledge by means of reading the writings of standard authors, both ancient and modern. He had great fondness for

the poets, having some talent in that direction himself. Among the colored poets he regarded Rev A. A.
Whitman as the chief ; and in his " Recollections of
Seventy Years," quotes from two of his works, " Not
a Man and Yet a Man," and the " Rape of Florida."
He read with keen interest every production of a colored author which he could get possession of, whether
a pamphlet or a book. He had made himself ac-
quainted with the works of such men as Bishops A.
W Wayman, H. M. Turner, B. T Tanner, Rev T. G
Steward, D D., and Prof. W S. Scarborough, A. M.,
LL.B. He was always delighted to take note of any literary accomplishment produced by a colored person,
however humble and unpretentious it might be. He
well knew how to appreciate the fact that " Tall oaks
from little acorns grow "

LITERARY PRODUCTIONS.

In view of his increased labors and travels for full
fifty years, and in consideration of the fact that he in-
habited an earthly tenement of clay which never
weighed one hundred pounds, the amount of literary
work which he was able to accomplish is simply
marvelous. In early life he began to practice the art
of writing both poetry and prose. He was a careful
and painstaking writer, and many of his productions

WILBERFORCE UNIVERSITY IN 1893.

are strongly marked with an apostolic tone. His first literary effort for publication was made in 1843, when he wrote five epistles on the "Education of the Ministry," which attracted wide-spread attention throughout the Church. April, 1866, he published a work called the "Semi-Centenary and Retrospection of the A. M. E. Church." In 1885 he issued his "Treatise on Domestic Education," which is divided into twenty chapters, with an introduction by Rev. R. S. Rust, D. D. It is a 24mo volume of 184 pages. It is full of thoughtful and valuable suggestions, and claims the attention of every parent. It concludes with this striking prediction:

"In the near future, from the well-disciplined Christian families shall issue the well-governed Christian Church and the well-governed Christian State; both existing, expanding, developing under the protection and guidance of unerring wisdom and omnipotent goodness, both perpetuating themselves till the nations shall be summoned before the Judge of all the earth, who is Lord of lords and King of kings. To whom be glory, honor, and dominion forever and ever. Amen.

In 1888 he brought out two works: "Recollections of Seventy Years," and a small volume containing the Quadrennial Sermon and the Ordination Sermon that he delivered at the General Conference of the A. M. E. Church in May of the same year.

His "Recollections of Seventy Years," is a 12mo
book of 335 pages with illustrations. It is full of interesting facts, and notes many important events in
the history of the colored people of America not to be
found in any other work. It acquaints the reader
with all the pioneer leaders of the colored people which
they furnished for their own deliverance. In fact, in
a certain sense, it is a manual of the history of the
colored people in general, and of the African Methodist Episcopal Church in particular. It also, in part.
records the doings of a large number of the early
abolitionists, who battled so heroically for the over-
throw of American slavery. It chronicles the author's
career from early childhood to the time of its publication. In a very large sense it is the autobiography of
Daniel Alexander Payne. He concludes with this
paragraph:

"But what will be the use of these recollections of men and
things; what of these reflections on them if they will not awaken
some slumbering boy ; if they fail to excite the latent faculties of a
sportive lad ; if they be not effective in stimulating the energies of
some youth, who, having strong, pure, good blood flowing from a
large, broad heart through his entire body, is by nature fitted to
accomplish good work for God in heaven and good things for man
on earth ? O youthful reader, hear me ! The spirit of Rev. John
Brown, of Haddington, Scotland, aroused my soul to a life of use-

fulness. Shall not my soul start thee on a career of study and usefulness that shall be pleasing to thy Creator, and that will bring
blessings to mankind?

> " For a useful life by holy wisdom crowned,
> Is all I ask, let weal or woe abound."

The two sermons referred to are master-pieces in
their line and are the only sermons of his which have
been published with his approval. Their delivery
produced a most profound impression upon the large
audiences that heard them. In 1852 he preached his
first sermon at the opening of a General Conference of
the A. M. E. Church, and in 1888, his last. Both of
the sermons which he delivered in 1888 are vigorous
in expression and ring with holy eloquence. I have
selected two excerpts to indicate the lofty character of
these two sermons. The first is from the Quadrennial
and the second from the Ordination :

" Then there are these two qualities which ought to be possessed
by every man, whether he be licentiate, deacon, elder, or bishop.
He must have the capacity to take in knowledge as a sponge ab-
sorbs water, and must make what he takes in a part of himself ;
must be active, and have capacity to develop his activity. He
must have a good memory, and what he learns must be engraved
on his heart; he must love it, live it, and then give it out with his
lips to the people. These are qualities which every man who de-
sires to be a minister should have. He should in all things emulate
the great Teacher. He should be crucified to the world and be

dead unto sin, but alive unto righteousness through Jesus Christ our Lord. He should be taught and instructed. He should be holy, and then will come upon him the Holy Ghost and the tongue of fire."

"Now the character of this spirit which always rested upon Jesus was the spirit of wisdom and understanding. These two accompanied him. They were not separated; they were linked in a single chain—wisdom and understanding. Not knowledge, for knowledge is not wisdom; not simple science, for that is not wisdom; not literature, for literature is not wisdom; not philosophy, for philosophy is not wisdom. What, then, is wisdom? It is power, the gift, the endowment to know how to use knowledge when acquired, how to interpret knowedge, how to apply knowledge, how to use it, and how and when to forbear using it. This is wisdom. It plans as God plans, and executes as God executes. Knowledge is only an instrument in the hand of wisdom, only the sword by which it fights and conquers, only the mode by which this thing and that thing and the other thing is known as resembling or differing one from another. Wisdom rises and towers as far above learning and talent as the heaven towers above the earth."

In 1891 he issued his last and greatest work—"The History of the A. M. E. Church from 1816 to 1856. It is an 8mo volume of 502 pages, embellished with four steel portraits and has the convenience of a copious index. He was appointed official historian of the A. M. E. Church in 1848, and this volume therefore, is the result of 43 years of research and investigation. It is the most valuable contribution that has

yet been made to the literature of the A. M. E.
Church. It is a standard work of information, and
as such needs no comment. As the author has
passed into the great beyond, it will, perhaps, not be
deemed inappropriate to reprint here the concluding
paragraphs of this matchless work.

"And now having completed the work as the historian of the
African Methodist Episcopal Church, the writer thinks it cannot
be finished with any better words than the command which the
Lord our God gave to Abraham : 'And when Abram was ninety
years old and nine, the Lord appeared to Abram, and said unto
him, I am the Almighty God : walk before me and be thou
perfect.'

" We cannot do better than to echo this command and say to all
—to every man, woman and child of the African Methodist Episcopal Church as individual elements in it, and to the aggregated
whole African M. E. Church : The Almighty God is the God who
has led thee on from one degree of strength to another, until thou
hast attained a little productive power. Do not be proud of it, for
pride does not become mortal man. Do not boast of it, for boast-
ing is the breath of pride. Remember that God looks at the proud
afar off. Rather be modest, be humble, be grateful, be obedient,
be loving, be faithful, and He, the Almighty God of Abraham,
Isaac and Jacob, will raise thee to a higher plane of strength, of
power, of usefulness, and consequent greatness. Listen to him, as
Abraham listened, when He says unto thee, 'African Methodist
Episcopal Church, I am the Almighty God : walk thou before me,
and be thou perfect.' 'Be thou perfect in every one of thy mem-

bers, be thou perfect in every one of thy departments, and I will
make thee to multiply exceedingly;' 'and I will make thee
exceedingly fruitful;' 'and I will establish my covenant between
me and thee and thy seed after thee in their generations, for an
everlasting covenant, to be a God unto thee and thy seed after
thee.' Listen A. M. E. Church, O, listen, and when thou hearest,
obey the command of the Lord God Almighty when He says,
'Walk before me and be thou perfect.' 'I have formed thee, and
I have led two generations of thine; I can, I will, I shall, lead a
thousand generations further and higher than I have led thee and
thine. Only walk before me as Abraham did, and with me as
Enoch did.' 'Fear not, I am thy shield and thy exceeding great
reward.' 'Walk before me and be thou perfect.'"

TRAVELS.

It may be said that he began his career as a traveler
when he left Charleston for New York in 1835. July,
1846, he started on a voyage to Europe as a delegate
to the organization of the "Evangelical Alliance,"
which took place in London. After the ship had been
five days out a terrible storm arose, which so disabled
it that it was compelled to return. From 1850 to 1852,
he was engaged in traveling through the Eastern
States in search of data for the History of the A. M. E.
Church. From 1852, the time when he was elected
to the Bishopric, until 1867, he traveled almost inces-
santly, extending the borders of the A. M. E. Church,
and soliciting funds for Wilberforce University.

May 8th, 1867, he set sail a second time for Europe,
on board the ship "Cuba," and after an uneventful voyage of ten days reached Liverpool.   He went to
Europe in the interest of Wilberforce University and
the mission work of the A. M. E. Church in the
South.   He had as fellow-passengers the noted abolitionists, Wm. Lloyd Garrison and George Thompson.
While in London, he visited St. Paul's Cathedral,
Westminster Abbey, the statue of Wilberforce, the
original Protection Society, the British Museum, and
the graves of Wesley, Clark, Benson and Watson.
He also attended a banquet which was given in honor
of Wm. Lloyd Garrison.

August 18th, he left London for Amsterdam, to be
present at the Fifth General Assembly of the Evangelical Alliance.   During his stay in Amsterdam he took
a side trip to Paris, where he spent three days, attend-
ing a meeting of the Anti-Slavery Conference. On the
adjournment of the Alliance he returned to Paris,
where he remained nearly a month. He then returned to London, where he spent the months of
September, October and November, when he went
once more to Paris and remained until the following April.   Leaving Paris he went to Liverpool, which place he reached on the 27th of the

same month, where he remained two days, and then embarked on " The City of Antwerp," on his return voyage home, and reached New York May 11th.

From 1867 to 1876 his travels were somewhat restricted, as he found it necessary to devote the larger measure of his time to Wilberforce University. From 1876 to 1880 he confined his travels chiefly to visiting the churches in the First Episcopal District, over which he had charge.

In 1880 he made a second trip to Europe as a delegate to the first Methodist Ecumenical Conference, which assembled September 7th, in London. He left New York on his second European voyage July 9th, reaching Liverpool on the morning of the 20th, thus giving himself about six weeks in Europe before the meeting of the Ecumenical Conference. He took advantage of the interval to revisit Paris, also to visit Canterbury, the Monastery of Fountains, Springs of Harrowgate, Glasgow, Edinburg and York.

September 21st, he left Liverpool for New York, which place he reached October 4th. From 1880 to the time of his death, he did but little traveling, spending his winters in Florida, availing himself of the mild and balmy climate of that section.

He spent the principal part of the winter of 1889-90

in his native city, which was the last visit he paid
to it.

The aggregate number of miles which he traveled
in his lifetime would reach away up into the hundred of thousands, and it is marvelous, in view of his
diminutive physical nature, how he endured the wear
and tear of such extensive travel.

AS A CITIZEN.

As a citizen he was loyal, law-abiding and interested in all that pertained to the prosperity of his
country. He took special interest in all movements
which were put forward for the triumph of universal
freedom and universal suffrage on American soil. He
was an earnest advocate of popular education, believ-
ing that the safety of the Republic depended upon the
enlightenment of its citizens, and that universal intelligence was the chief tower of strength of universal freedom. He was also interested in public chari-
ties, and was always ready to give his counsel and
financial aid to any worthy cause for the establishment
of such. He took no special interest in politics outside of what pertained to the duties of citizenship, be-
lieving that the field of statesmanship should be left
to those who were trained for that calling. In 1835 he
had the first opportunity of visiting a public assembly,

which was the anniversary of the American Anti-slavery Society, held in New York City. Here he heard the noted abolitionist, Lewis Tappan, pleading for the publication of a small pamphlet to be called " The Child's Anti-Slavery Magazine." He argued "that all children are naturally anti-slavery and that it is only by a training, as false as it is wicked, that they become pro-slavery."

In 1862 he had an interview with President Lincoln on the day following the passage, by Congress, of the bill abolishing slavery in the District of Columbia. The object of this interview was to learn, if possible, whether the President intended to sign it. Senator Washburn, of Illinois, and Senator Carl Schurz, of Missouri, were present at the time. The President was non-committal. Bishop Payne said, "Mr. President, you will remember that on the eve of your departure from Springfield, Ill., you begged the citizens of the Republic to pray for you." He said, " Yes." Bishop Payne then remarked, " From that moment, we, the colored citizens of the Republic, have been praying: ' O Lord just as Thou didst cause the throne of David to wax stronger and stronger, while that of Saul waxed weaker and weaker ; so, we beseech Thee, cause the power at Washington to grow stronger and stronger, and that at Richmond to grow weaker and weaker.' "

October, 1864, he attended a meeting of the National Freedman's Aid Commission in Philadelphia. Among the speakers were the Rt. Rev. Bishop McIlvain, of Ohio, who was its president; Dr. Bellows, Bishop Simpson, Rev. Henry Ward Beecher, and William Lloyd Garrison. It was an important meeting. It was generally feared that when the troops were withdrawn from the South, the school teachers who went there from the North to instruct the freedmen would be expelled. It was also urged that all the civil rights of the freedman should be recognized by congressional legislation before the rebel states were admitted into the Union. The consensus of opinion on this point was unanimous and emphatic, as Connecticut had already refused to grant the elective franchise to her colored citizens. The question of Southern outrages was also discussed, and, owing to certain reports which had been given out, it was feared that the condition of the freedmen would be but little removed from that of actual servitude. Bishop Payne was intensely interested in the proceedings of the Commission, and his suggestions and advice doubtless had some bearing on its final

conclusion. This is referred to as proof that he never
lost sight of the material interests of his people. In
this particular he followed in the footsteps of his il-
lustrious predecessors who, with many of his distinguished contemporaries and himself, constituted a
power in the land when the battle waged fiercely between freedom and oppression. These all stood for
liberty, justice and equal rights.

HOME LIFE.

He was twice married. His first wife, whom he
married in 1847, was the widowed daughter of Mr.
William Becraft, of Georgetown, D. C. Her widowed
name was Mrs. Julia A. Ferris. She died within a
year after their marriage. Her babe, a daughter, sur-
vived her only about nine months, when she was
called to join her sainted mother in the spirit world.
Bishop Payne felt the blow of this affliction very
keenly, and he cherished the memory of his first wife
and infant daughter through all the years of subsequent life.

In the summer of 1853, he married the second
time. As was his first wife, so was his second, a wid-
ow—Mrs. Eliza J. Clark, of Cincinnati, O. She had
three children by her first husband living at the time

"EVERGREEN COTTAGE" IN 1889.

of her second marriage—John Alexander, Laura and Augusta Eva.

In 1856, he moved to Tawawa Springs, O., now Wilberforce, where he continued to reside until the close of his earthly career. His chief reason for removing from Cincinnati to Tawawa Springs was to secure for his step-children the advantages of instruction under the care of competent Christian teachers. In referring to this in his " Recollections of Seventy Years," he says: " I believed, I hoped, I prayed that they would develop characters that would render them at the very least respectable and useful members of society." In this he was not disappointed.

When Wilberforce University passed into the control of the A. M. E. Church, Bishop Payne moved into one of the cottages on the campus. Subsequently he secured a piece of ground outside of it, on which he erected an elegant home, and which he named " Evergreen Cottage." This was a model home. The rooms are large and airy, well lighted and ventilated, and were comfortably, but not gorgeously furnished. The grounds were well laid off and kept with scrupulous care. The Bishop took great delight in cultivating shrubbery and vines and in keeping the evergreens which adorned the front-yard neatly trimmed.

The evergreens were the objects of his special concern and care. For years he had watched their growth and development with keen interest; and when, in 1889, the serious, and, finally, fatal illness of Mrs. Payne seemed to demand their removal, he gave his consent with great reluctance. When the evergreens and vines were removed he was heard to say that "Evergreen Cottage" existed only in name. The whole place gave evidence of solid comfort. It was the home of a man who knew how to live wisely and well. It was not the recluse of a hermit, nor the cell of a stolid friar, but the abode of a genial, cheerful, liberal soul. All who have had the pleasure of being entertained in that home will gladly bear testimony to the fact that Bishop Payne's hospitality was unbounded. He always delighted to have with him persons of intelligence and culture. He was a born gentleman, possessed of æsthetic tastes and qualities which made him a fit companion even for kings and princes. He was as polite as a Chesterfield, and no one was more chaste or pure in language than he. He detested boorishness, and everything whether an act or an expression, which had the least semblance of vulgarity, profanity or irreverence. It was a pleasure and an inspiration to enjoy his association. As a con-

"EVERGREEN COTTAGE" IN 1893.

versationalist, he was instructive, entertaining and interesting. His words and sayings were those of a seer,
and never failed to command the attention of the most
erudite.

As might be expected, books, magazines and papers
were to be found in his home in abundance. He possessed a large and valuable library. He was a sub-
scriber to a number of magazines published in Europe.
It was his custom for many years to assemble the
members of his household in the library after tea to
hear his wife read from the daily press the leading
items of current news, in which he took great interest.
He has remarked frequently that she was the best
reader not possessed of a scholastic education he had
ever heard. He would allow no one else to perform
that service if her duties would permit her to do so.
His home was well-ordered and established, and from
its altar morning and evening, the incense of prayer
and praise arose to the Father of all the families of
the earth. His second wife, familiarly known for a
number of years as "Mamma Payne," died in 1889.
Two of his step-children survive him—John Alexander Clark, the father of Edward, Laura and Ella
Clark—all of whom were educated at Wilberforce and
became teachers—and Augusta Eva, the wife of Rev. J.

H. Jones, now pastor of St. Paul A. M. E. church,
Columbus. Since the death of Mrs. Payne, Miss
Laura was his chief attendant, and she smoothed the
pillow upon which his head was laid when he yielded
up the ghost and died. She is a noble young woman
of pure and spotless character.

MORAL AND RELIGIOUS CHARACTER.

The task of chronicling anything like a correct esti-
mate of his moral and religious character will require
more time and resources than I can now command.
He was a pure and conscientious Christian, and his life
was a living epistle to be read and known by all men.
The law as given by God to Moses on Mount Sinai
was his code of Moral Ethics. He believed that every
word and line of the Decalogue was intended to govern
men in their motives, thought, speech and conduct.
He constantly admonished those who came under his
instruction to clothe themselves with all the moral
virtues. At one time, in speaking of the spirit of might,
which was an element in Christ's manhood, he said,
" It is moral excellence and purity of thought, uncontaminated by filth and rot, moving among the impure
as the archangel moves among them, uncontaminated
and untainted. This is moral might and purity. It
comes down from heaven only to save, not to be con-

taminated. Let us strive then to bring moral might up to its high and pure position." He argued that the moral man is also spiritual minded and that the great strength of the spiritual comes from the moral. I feel free to venture the assertion that he was a model of the perfect moral man. During his long and eventful life, not even the breath of a suspicion to the contrary was directed against him.

His religion was of the Pauline type—consistent, heroic and aggressive. He was given to much prayer, meditation and reading of the Scriptures. He recognized his absolute dependence upon divine grace to enable him to keep in the path of righteousness and holy living. He constantly sought the unction and power of the Holy Spirit. So deep and fervent was his piety, and so potent his spirituality, that Bishop Grant was led to make the remark that "he is living on earth and in heaven at the same time, and he will have a foretaste of the joys and bliss of the latter place before entering it."

He possessed humility coupled with courage. He had great boldness when it was necessary to defend the truth and right. At times, he would seem to glow with righteous indignation when making an attack on wickedness and sin.

In describing the qualifications of the minister, among other things, he was wont to say. that " The minister should be humble-minded and be an example to all believers that they might imitate the Lord Jesus Christ. That he should be careful that the words coming from his lips be in harmony with the spirit of holiness, and that in his dealing with the people his conduct ought to be in harmony with the Spirit of the Living God, as becomes a humble man and teacher of his brethren."

The following is a part of the message he delivered to Miss Laura Clark, just previous to his dissolution :

" At the point of eighty-three, I still find it to be eternally true that the curse of God is upon the house of the wicked. It is not said that it *shall be* or *will be* ; but that is *now* upon the house of the wicked, and His blessings upon the just from generation to generation. The divine statements are not made upon the speculations of science nor the fore-knowledge of prophecies ; but upon facts which must remain true for all coming ages. To sustain these remarks examine Deuteronomy chapter iv, and chapter x from 23rd verse. Genesis chapters iv and vi. Psalms cxii, first three verses. Therefore, stand firm for that which is true, that which is good ; and hesitate not to handle the two edged sword in cutting off and cutting down the evil."

The force of his religious and moral character remains as a goodly heritage to the Church of his choice; and, in the years to come, it will be said of

FLORAL OFFERINGS AT WILBERFORCE.

him, as it was said of the martyr, Stephen, " He was a good man, and full of the Holy Ghost."

FUNERAL SERVICES.

The funeral services of Bishop Payne, both at Wilberforce and Baltimore, were quiet, impressive and imposing. At Wilberforce eulogies were delivered by President S. T. Mitchell, Rev. J G. Mitchell, D. D., Bishops Turner and Tanner, and Mr. William Anderson. The chapel was appropriately draped. The floral offerings were unique and attractive, especially the design of a clock. Aside from the faculty, students and members of the community, there was a large attendance of preachers and citizens resident elsewhere. It was a stormy day and the ground was covered with snow.

At Baltimore there were large delegations from Philadelphia and Washington. A most excellent and impressive funeral discourse was delivered by Bishop Wayman. Brief eulogistic addresses were made by Bishop Handy, Mrs. Fannie Jackson-Coppin, and the writer. The Rev. Dr. J. W Beckett, the pastor of Bethel Church, Rev. Dr. J. C. Embry, and the Rev. Theodore Gould, assisted in the services. Dr. Beckett sang a solo full of pathos and sweetness. Resolutions from the Baltimore Preachers' Meeting were read by

Rev. Mr Hurst. The writer, acting in behalf of the
Sunday School Union, presented two floral emblems
—a large pillow with the motto, "At rest," and a
sheaf of ripened wheat. A handsome wreath was presented by the Baltimore Preachers' Meeting.

By a singular coincidence the day was as stormy at
Baltimore as it had been at Wilberforce the preced-
ing Sunday, and a mantle of snow covered the ground.
The appearance of snow both at Wilberforce and Baltimore seemed to indicate that nature was in harmony
with Bishop Payne's request that his shroud should be
made of white woolen cloth. This request was con-
formed to, and the lifeless form of the distinguished
prelate lay in a handsome casket robed in white. Presiding Elder W H. Brown, of the Pittsburg Conference, Rev. Mr. Gowens, of Baltimore, and the writer,
were the watchers during the night the body rested in
Bethel Church. The body was accompanied from Wilberforce to Baltimore by Bishops Wayman, Arnett,
Salter and Handy; President S. T. Mitchell, Dr. J. G.
Mitchell, Prof. J. P Shorter, Presiding Elder Brown,
of the Pittsburg Conference, the writer, and the members of the family—Rev and Mrs. J. H. Jones, Miss
Laura E. Clark and Master Clarence Clark. Mrs.
John Alexander Clark joined the family at Baltimore.

Bishop Tanner, Drs. Coppin and Heard accompanied the body from Wilberforce to Harrisburg, where they continued their journey to Philadelphia. The body was placed in a vault to await interment in the Spring.

Concluding, it may be said, the lamp of his earthly existence has been extinguished forever. He will no more speak in human language to the children of men, while his spirit has returned to the God who gave it. But, he is not dead! No, not even sleeps! Seventy-four years a student, sixty-four years an educator, fifty years a preacher, and forty-one years a Bishop, his name and fame are secure, and his memory is imperishable, being incarnated in the active and widespreading influences for good and blessedness which he so nobly created and so heroically sustained.

> " Servant of God, well done!
> Rest from thy loved employ :
> The battle fought, the vict'ry won,
> Enter thy Master's joy."

www.ingramcontent.com/pod-product-compliance
Lightning Source LLC
Chambersburg PA
CBHW021228260626
47172CB00002B/658